When God made the world,
he formed all kinds of creatures,
Fashioned in families of similar features.

A Gaggle of Geese & a Clutter of Cats

Dandi Daley Mackall
illustrated by David Hohn

WATERBROOK
PRESS

A Gaggle of Geese and a Clutter of Cats
Published by WaterBrook Press
12265 Oracle Boulevard, Suite 200
Colorado Springs, Colorado 80921
A division of Random House Inc.

All Scripture quotations are taken from the Holy Bible, New Living Translation, Copyright ©
1996, 2004. Used by permission of Tyndale House Publishers Inc., Wheaton, Illinois 60189.
All rights reserved.

ISBN 978-1-4000-7204-0

Copyright © 2007 by Dandi Daley Mackall
Illustrations © 2007 by David Hohn

Library of Congress Cataloging-in-Publication Data
Mackall, Dandi Daley
A gaggle of geese and a clutter of cats / by Dandi Daley Mackall ; [illustrations by David
Hohn]. — 1st ed.
    p. cm. — (Dandilion rhymes)
Summary: Introduces in rhyming text the collective names used for various animal groups.
ISBN 978-1-4000-7204-0
[1. Animals—Nomenclature—Fiction. 2. English language—Collective nouns—Fiction.
3. Christian life—Fiction. 4. Stories in rhyme.] I. Hohn, David, 1974– ill. II. Title.
PZ8.3.M179Gag 2007
[E]—dc22

                              2007004960

Printed in China
2007—First Edition

10 9 8 7 6 5 4 3 2 1

Everyone knows there are kittens in **litters**,
Packs, **flocks**, and **herds**, common names
for our critters.
But animal groups go by fancy names, too,
In jungles, a pet store, a pasture, or zoo.

So what's in a name of an animal group?

A **muster** of peacocks,

A kangaroo **troop**,

A fine **flock** of chickens,
A hedgehog **array**?

When squirrels get together, we call
it a DRAY.

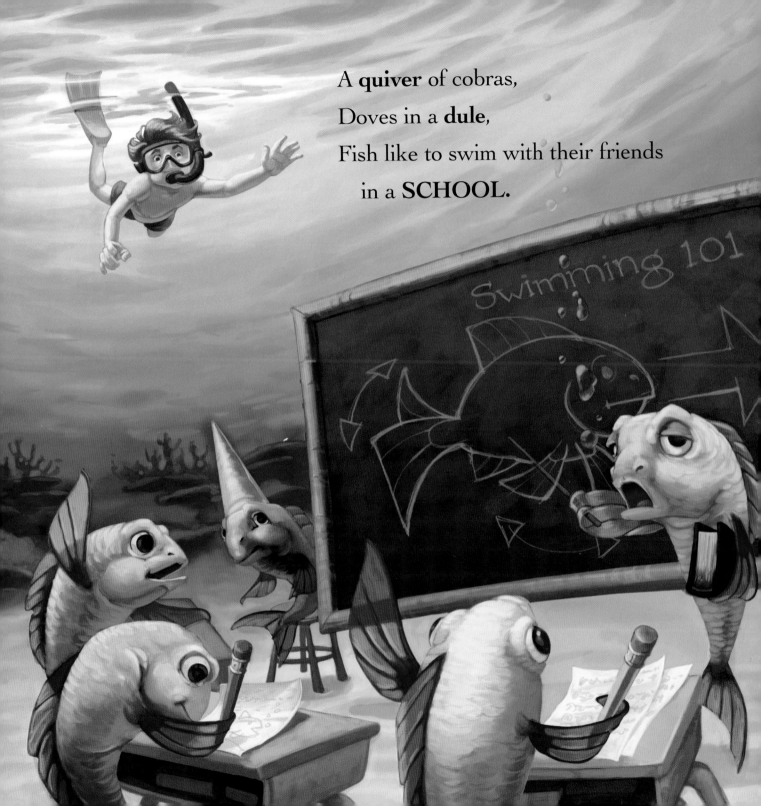

A **quiver** of cobras,
Doves in a **dule**,
Fish like to swim with their friends
in a **SCHOOL**.

Swimming 101

An **aerie** of eagles,
A jellyfish **smack**,

A **skulk** of wild foxes,
And wolves in a **PACK**.

But what are these crows called?
Please tell me! Who knows?

Just peek in their nest —
It's a **MURDER** of
crows!

A **colony** of beavers,
An **army** of frogs,

A **gaggle** of geese,

And a **DRIFT** of fat hogs.

But what will you find if you follow
this trail?
A group of these creatures—

A **BEVY** of quail!

An **unkindness** of ravens,

A **mischief** of rats,

A **shrewdness** of apes,

And a **CLUTTER** of cats.

Like whales and like walruses,
Though it sounds odd,
All dolphins and porpoises swim in a **POD**.

A large **leap** of leopards,
A **pod** of brown seals,

A **pride** of brave lions,

A **swarm** of six eels.

A group of these bears—
And I'm telling the truth—
When they get together, we call it a **SLEUTH**.

A **rookery** of penguins is more than just two.

A **hoard** of new hamsters,

A **herd** of gnu.

Put ten toads together, and what
    have you got?
A grouping of toads, you can call it
    a **KNOT**.

Tidings of magpies,

Ducks in a **brace**,

Elks in a **gang**—in a galloping race.

Listen! A gobble!

Get ready for laughter.

A group of wild turkeys, we call it a **RAFTER**.

Owls in a **parliament**,
Snakes in a **bed**,

A **CRASH** of rhinoceroses, very well fed.

Now here's a fine group. What's the name?

Please keep guessing!

A big group of kids?

Why, we call them a **BLESSING!**

"And God said, 'Let the waters swarm with fish and other life. Let the skies be filled with birds of every kind.' So God created great sea creatures and every sort of fish and every kind of bird. And God saw that it was good…. And God said, 'Let the earth bring forth every kind of animal—livestock, small animals, and wildlife.' And so it was. God made all sorts of wild animals, livestock, and small animals, each able to reproduce more of its own kind. And God saw that it was good."

—GENESIS 1:20-25 (NLT)